And the Puppies

Adaptation from the animated series: Carine Laforest
Illustrations taken from the animated series and adapted by Mario Allard

Caillou and Daddy went to Mr. Hinkle's to help him build a dog house.
"I'm so glad you could come and help!" said Mr. Hinkle.
"Hello, Mr. Hinkle. Where's the doggy?" Caillou asked.
"There are not just one but three dogs! Two puppies and a mommy," said Mr. Hinkle.

Caillou heard a soft bark.
"That's one of the pups. I think he wants to meet you."
A little dog appeared behind the screen door. Then
two other dogs showed up. "One puppy, two puppy,
three doggies!"
"Would you like to play with them?" asked Mr. Hinkle.

Caillou wanted to play with the puppies, but he wasn't sure.
Sometimes he felt nervous around dogs.
'Come closer, Caillou. Let me introduce you to Mimi."
Mr. Hinkle opened the door, and the dog came to sit next to him.
'That's a good girl, Mimi! She's the mommy," Mr. Hinkle said.

"You can let her get to know you by stroking her side, not her head," explained Mr. Hinkle.
Caillou gently petted Mimi's side.
"Hello, Mimi." Mimi licked Caillou's hand. Then her tail started wagging.
"She likes you!" said Daddy. Caillou felt a little better.

Caillou was still a bit nervous, but he liked the puppies very much. They were so full of energy! The puppies kept running around Caillou, and the boldest one darted between his legs.
"Whoa!" Caillou almost fell down.
Daddy laughed. "They're very excited about playing with you," said Daddy.

One of the pups disappeared. "Where did the spotty puppy go?" Caillou asked. "He can't be far," replied Mr. Hinkle. "I bet he's hiding."
"I'll go and find him!" Caillou exclaimed. Caillou ran to the backyard, followed by the chocolate puppy.

"Here, puppy!" called Caillou. He got on his knees
to look inside a bush.
It didn't take long for the chocolate puppy to jump
on Caillou's back and start licking his face. It tickled!

"Come on puppy, we need to find your brother,"
Caillou giggled.

Caillou heard the spotty puppy barking.
"Where are you hiding?"
Caillou saw him dash through an opening in the hedge.
The puppy was playing hide-and-seek, one of Caillou's
favorite games. He followed the pup through the gap.
"There you are!" Caillou exclaimed, as the puppy ran
back into Mr. Hinkle's yard.

Caillou ran back to Daddy and Mr. Hinkle.
"Have you seen the puppy?"
"We haven't seen him," answered Mr. Hinkle.
"Help us put this roof on, and then we'll help
you look for the dog."
Daddy and Mr. Hinkle lifted the roof. "There
he is!" exclaimed Caillou. "The puppy was
hiding under the roof."

Daddy and Mr. Hinkle were done assembling the dog house. It just needed a final touch.

"Caillou, would you like to help us decorate the doghouse?"

Daddy handed Caillou the screwdriver and held a screw in place.

"Make sure the screws are on tight."

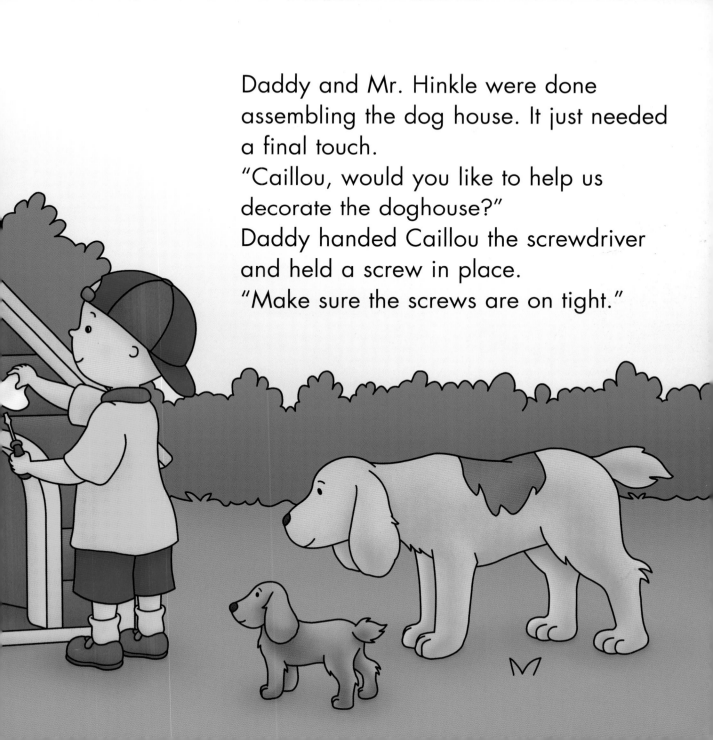

"It's a great house!" said Caillou. "Come here, Mimi! C'mon, puppies!" called Mr. Hinkle. The dogs settled comfortably inside their new home. "They like the house, Mr. Hinkle," said Caillou. One of the puppies hopped into Caillou's lap and yawned. "I think the puppies like you, too!" said Daddy.

Text: adaptation by Carine Laforest of the animated series CAILLOU,
produced by DHX Media Inc.
All rights reserved.
Original story written by Andrew Chappell
Original Episode #88: Caillou and the Puppies
Illustrations: Mario Allard, based on the animated series CAILLOU
Coloration: Eric Lehouillier

The PBS KIDS logo is a registered mark of PBS and is used with permission.

Chouette Publishing would like to thank the Government of Canada and SODEC
for their financial support.

Books
Tax Credit

Gestion
SODEC

Catalogage avant publication de Bibliothèque et Archives nationales
du Québec et Bibliothèque et Archives Canada

Laforest, Carine, 1967-
Caillou and the puppies

(Clubhouse)
For children aged 2 to 6.

ISBN 978-2-89718-445-2

1. Caillou (Fictitious character) - Juvenile literature. 2. Puppies - Juvenile literature.
I. Allard, Mario, 1969-   . II. Title. III. Series: Clubhouse.

SF426.5.L33 2017   j636.7   C2016-942548-7

Printed in China
10 9 8 7 6 5 4 3 2 1   CHO2004 MAY2017